Hiding Heidi

For Martin

little bee books

A division of Bonnier Publishing | 853 Broadway, New York, New York 10003

Manufactured in China TL 0316
First Edition 10 9 8 7 6 5 4 3 2 1
Library of Congress Cataloging-in-Publication Data is available upon request.
ISBN 978-1-4998-0350-1
littlebeebooks.com
bonnierpublishing.com

Hiding Heidi

by Fiona Woodcock

little bee books

Heidi has a special talent.

Look!
She's doing it again!

Heidi can't help it.

Wherever she goes and
whatever she does,
it just happens.

Sometimes Heidi's friends join in.
They're good at hiding too.

But not as good as Heidi.
No one's as good at hiding as she is.
She's a natural.

One day, Heidi was hanging out with her friends.
"Let's have a hippity-hop race!" said Freddie.
"No, let's have a roller-skate race!" said Katie.
"No, no, no, let's not have a race at all," said Lizzie.
"Let's play on the jungle gym!"

They couldn't agree.

So in the end, they all played hide-and-seek.

Which Heidi won, of course.

The next day was Heidi's birthday.
All her friends came over for a party.
Everyone was dancing and having a lot of fun.

When the music stopped, Heidi giggled.
"*Now* can we play hide-and-seek?"

Heidi went off to hide.
Her friends searched for her high . . .

. . . and low.

But they couldn't find her.

They did, however, find some
delicious ice cream sundaes.

It wasn't until the very end of Heidi's party that she came out of her hiding spot and joined her friends.

"Sorry, Heidi. We couldn't find you, and we got tired of playing hide-and-seek."

Now her party was over, and Heidi thought . . .

and thought . . .

and thought.

The next day Heidi and her friends were hanging out.
"Let's have a hippity-hop race!" said Freddie.

"Yes, let's!" said Heidi quickly,
before anyone else could say a word.

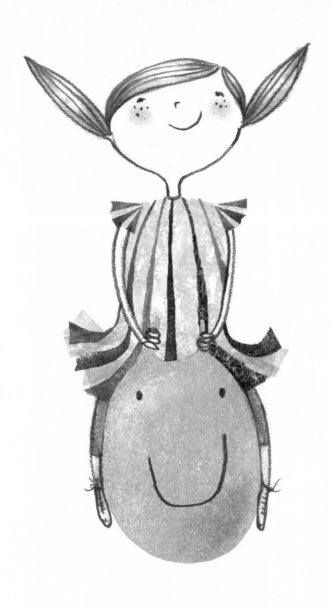

So they did.

Freddie was fantastic at bouncing.

Then they had a roller-skate race. With ribbons!
Katie was sensational at skating.

Then they clambered on the jungle gym.
Lizzie was incredible at climbing.

"See?" said Heidi as they all relaxed later.
"We don't ALWAYS have to play hide-and-seek. . . ."